Best-Loved
Aesop's Fables
Coloring Book

Maggie Swanson

DOVER PUBLICATIONS, INC.
Mineola, New York

Who wins the race—the tortoise or the hare? Which is stronger—the North Wind or the Sun? Why did no one pay attention to the boy who cried, "Wolf! Wolf!"? You'll find out when you read the entertaining tales in this delightful coloring book. The twenty-two fables—stories with a message that feature a variety of animal and human characters—were believed to have been written many years ago by a man named Aesop. Whether or not this is true, it's a fact that the stories contain words of wisdom in the "moral" at the end of each fable. Enjoy the fables, and have fun coloring in the pages as well.

Bibliographical Note
Best-Loved Aesop's Fables Coloring Book is a new work,
first published by Dover Publications, Inc., in 2015.

International Standard Book Number
ISBN-13: 978-0-486-79747-2
ISBN-10: 0-486-79747-3

Manufactured in the United States by RR Donnelley
79747301   2015
www.doverpublications.com

Best-Loved
Aesop's Fables
Coloring Book

The Hare and the Tortoise

One day, the Hare was laughing at the Tortoise for his slow and ungainly walk, so the Tortoise challenged him to a race. The Hare, looking on the whole affair as a great joke, agreed, and the Fox was selected to act as umpire and hold the stakes. The race began, and the Hare, of course, soon left the Tortoise far behind. When she reached midway to the finish line, she began to play and nibble the young grass and amuse herself in many ways. Because the day was so warm, she even thought she would take a little nap in a shady spot; even if the Tortoise should pass her while she slept, she could easily overtake him again before he reached the end. The Tortoise, however, plodded steadily on, unwavering and unresting, straight toward the finish line. Meanwhile, the Hare woke up suddenly from her nap, and was surprised to find that the Tortoise was nowhere in sight. Off she went at full speed, but when she got to the finish, she found that the Tortoise was already there, waiting for her arrival.

MORAL: *Slow and steady wins the race.*

The Fox and the Stork

One day a Fox invited a Stork to dine with him, and, deciding to play a joke on the Stork, he put the soup that he had for dinner in a large flat dish. Although the Fox himself could lap it up quite well, the Stork could only dip in the tips of his long bill. Some time after, the Stork, remembering the Fox's trick, invited him to dinner. He, in his turn, put some minced meat in a long, narrow-necked jar, into which he could easily put his bill, while the Fox was forced to be content licking what ran down the sides of the jar. The Fox then remembered his old trick, and had to admit that the Stork had paid him back in his own coin.

MORAL: *Don't complain when others treat you as you treat them.*

The Town Mouse and the Country Mouse

A Country Mouse, a plain, sensible sort of fellow, was once visited by a former companion of his, who had moved to a neighboring city. The Country Mouse put before his friend some fine peas, some choice bacon, and a bit of rare old Stilton cheese, and told him to enjoy his dinner. The City Mouse nibbled a little here and there in a dainty manner, wondering at the pleasure his host took in such plain and ordinary food. After dinner, the Town Mouse said to the Country Mouse, "Really, my good friend, how can you be happy in this dismal, boring place? You go on and on, in a dull humdrum sort of way, from one year's end to another. Come with me, this very night, and see with your own eyes what a life I lead." The Country Mouse agreed, and as soon as it was dark, off they started for the city, where they arrived just as a splendid supper given by the master of the house where our town friend lived was over. The City Mouse soon got together a heap of dainties on a corner of the handsome dinner table. The Country Mouse, who had never even heard the names of half the meats set before him, was wondering where to begin, when the door creaked, opened, and in came a servant with a light. The companions ran off, but as soon as it was quiet again, they returned to their dinner. Once more the door opened, and the son of the master of the house came in with a great bounce, followed by his little dog, who ran sniffing to the very spot where our friends had just been. The City Mouse was by that time safe in his hole—which, by the way, he had not been thoughtful enough to show to his friend, who had to hide behind a sofa, where he waited in fear and trembling until it was quiet again. The City Mouse then called upon him to finish his supper, but the Country Mouse said, "No, no; I'm leaving as fast as I can. I would rather have a crust of bread with peace and quiet than all your fine things in the middle of such alarms and frights as these."

MORAL: *A simple life without worries is better than a rich life full of cares.*

The Lapdog and the Donkey

A donkey noticed how his master enjoyed playing with his little lapdog, and he thought his master might like him to act the same way. So one day he leaned his heavy front hoofs on his master's shoulders and began to lick his master's face with his big, rough tongue. His master had to call the servants to drive him away.

MORAL: *Always be yourself and do not foolishly imitate others.*

The Fox and the Grapes

One day a hungry Fox saw some tempting Grapes hanging high up from the ground. He made many attempts to reach them, but all in vain. Tired out by his failures, he walked off grumbling to himself, "They are sour, anyway, and not at all fit for eating."

MORAL: *When people can't get what they want because of their own inabilities, they often pretend they didn't want it anyway.*

The Dog and His Shadow

A Dog, carrying in his mouth a piece of meat that he had stolen, was about to cross a stream. Looking down, he saw what he thought was another dog carrying another piece of meat. Snapping greedily to get this as well, he dropped the meat that he had, and lost it in the stream.

MORAL: *Be satisfied with what you have.*

Belling the Cat

A certain Cat that lived in a large house was so vigilant and active, that the Mice held a large meeting to consider what to do. Many plans had been presented and dismissed, when a young Mouse, rising and catching the eye of the president, said that he had a proposal to make, which he was sure would meet with the approval of everyone. "If," he said, "the Cat wore a little bell around her neck, every step she took would make it tinkle; then, always warned of her approach, we would have time to reach our holes. This way, we could live in safety, and defy her power." The speaker resumed his seat with a complacent air, and a murmur of applause arose from the audience. An old grey Mouse, with a twinkle in his eye, then got up, and said that the young Mouse's plan was admirable, but that it had one drawback: Who should put the bell around the Cat's neck?

MORAL: *It is easier to propose a plan than to put it into action.*

The Rooster and the Jewel

As a Rooster was scratching up the straw in a farmyard in search of food, he found a beautiful Jewel. "Ho!" he said, "you are a very fine thing, I'm sure, to those who prize you; but give me a barley-corn before all the pearls in the world."

MORAL: *Beauty without usefulness is sometimes undesirable.*

The Boy and the Figs

A Boy once thrust his hand into a jar full of figs and nuts. He grasped as many as his fist could possibly hold, but when he tried to take it out, the narrowness of the jar's neck prevented him. Not liking to lose any of them, but unable to take out his hand, he burst into tears and bitterly cried over his bad luck. An honest fellow who stood nearby gave him this wise and reasonable advice: "Grasp only half the quantity, my boy, and you will easily succeed."

MORAL: *Greed often hinders success.*

The Wind and the Sun

A dispute once arose between the North Wind and the Sun as to which was the stronger of the two. Seeing a traveler on his way, they agreed that whichever could make him take off his cloak first was the strongest. The North Wind began, and sent a furious blast, which nearly tore the cloak from its fastenings; but the traveler, seizing the garment with a firm grip, held it round his body so tightly that the Wind failed in his efforts. The Sun, scattering the clouds that had gathered, then darted his warmest beams on the traveler's head. Growing faint with the heat, the man flung off his cloak, and ran for protection to the nearest shade.

MORAL: *Persuasion is better than force, and a kind and gentle manner will get quicker results than threats.*

The Wind and the Sun

A dispute once arose between the North Wind and the Sun as to which was the stronger of the two. Seeing a traveler on his way, they agreed that whichever could make him take off his cloak first was the strongest. The North Wind began, and sent a furious blast, which nearly tore the cloak from its fastenings; but the traveler, seizing the garment with a firm grip, held it round his body so tightly that the Wind failed in his efforts. The Sun, scattering the clouds that had gathered, then darted his warmest beams on the traveler's head. Growing faint with the heat, the man flung off his cloak, and ran for protection to the nearest shade.

MORAL: *Persuasion is better than force, and a kind and gentle manner will get quicker results than threats.*

The Kid and the Wolf

A Kid, standing safely on a high rock, began to insult and jeer at a Wolf on the ground below. The Wolf, looking up, replied, "Do not think, vain creature, that you annoy me. I regard your insults as coming not from you, but from the place upon which you stand."

MORAL: *It's easy to be brave when you're far from danger.*

The Dove and the Ant

An Ant going to a river to drink fell in and was carried along in the stream. A Dove pitied her condition, and threw a stick into the river, which helped the Ant get to shore. Soon afterwards, the Ant saw a man with a gun aiming at the Dove. Just as he was about to fire, the Ant stung him in the foot and made him miss his aim, so saving the Dove's life.

MORAL: *One good turn deserves another.*

The Vinegrower and His Sons

An old vinegrower was about to die, and he wanted his sons to learn his trade. He called them to his bedside and said, "Boys, I'm dying. Find all there is in my vineyard." They thought there was a treasure hidden there, and after their father died they took picks and shovels and dug up all the ground eagerly. They found no treasure, but the ground had been very well prepared for the vines, which produced a huge number of grapes and made them rich.

MORAL: *Hard work is man's greatest treasure.*

The Young Mouse, the Rooster and the Cat

A young Mouse, returning to his hole after leaving it for the first time, related his adventures to his mother: "Mother," he said, "I rambled about today like a Young Mouse of spirit, who wished to see and to be seen, when two such amazing creatures came my way! One was so gracious, so gentle and kind! The other, who was noisy and forbidding, had on his head and under his chin, pieces of raw meat, which shook at every step he took. Then, all at once, he began beating his sides with the utmost fury and let out such a harsh and piercing cry that I ran away in terror, just as I was about to introduce myself to the other stranger. She was covered with fur like our own, only richer-looking and much more beautiful, and she seemed so modest and benevolent that it made me feel good just to look at her." "Ah, my son," replied the Old Mouse, "learn while you can to distrust appearances. The first strange creature was nothing but a Rooster, that will soon be killed, and when he's put on a dish in the pantry, we may have a delicious supper. The other was a nasty, sly, and bloodthirsty hypocrite of a Cat, who likes nothing to eat so well as a young and juicy little Mouse like yourself!"

MORAL: *Don't be deceived by grand appearances.*

The Boy Who Cried Wolf

Once there was a mischievous Boy who used to watch over a flock of sheep near a village. As a joke, the Boy used to cry out, "Wolf! Wolf!" in order to see all the Villagers rush to his aid. When they discovered that there was no Wolf, the Boy just laughed at them. One day, after the Boy had tricked the Villagers several times, a Wolf really did appear. But this time, when the Boy cried, "Wolf! Wolf!" the Villagers, who were tired of being laughed at, ignored his cries for help, and the whole flock was lost.

MORAL: *If you tell a lot of lies, no one will believe you even when you tell the truth.*

The Fox and the Woodman

A Fox being chased by some Hunters came up to a man who was cutting wood, and begged him for a place to hide. The man showed him his own hut, and the Fox crept in and hid himself in a corner. The Hunters presently came up and asked the man whether he had seen the Fox. "No," he replied, but at the same time, he pointed his finger to the corner. They, however, did not understand the hint and were off again immediately. When the Fox perceived that they were out of sight, he was stealing off without saying a word. But the man stopped him, saying, "Is this the way you leave your host, without a word of thanks for your safety?" "A pretty host!" said the Fox, turning round upon him. "If you had been as honest with your fingers as you were with your tongue, I would not have left without saying goodbye."

MORAL: *Actions speak louder than words.*

The Fortune Teller

A Man who claimed to be a Wizard and Fortune teller, used to stand in the marketplace and pretend to tell fortunes, give information about missing property and other similar things. One day, while he was busily going about his business, a mischievous fellow broke through the crowd, and gasping as if he were out of breath, told him that his house was on fire and would shortly burn to the ground. At the news, the Wizard ran off as fast as his legs could carry him, while the Joker and a crowd of other people followed at his heels. But the house, it seems, was not on fire at all, and the Joker then asked him, amid the jeers of the people, how could he, who was so clever at telling other people's fortunes, know so little of his own?

MORAL: *Those who practice deception are often most easily deceived.*

The Peacock and the Crane

The Peacock, spreading his gorgeous tail, strutted up and down in his most stately manner before a Crane, and laughed at him for his plain feathers. "Tut, tut!" said the Crane; "which is better, to strut about in the dirt, and be gazed at by children, or to soar above the clouds, as I do?"

MORAL: *Those who are most conceited often have the least cause.*

The Old Man and His Sons

An Old Man had many Sons who were always quarrelling with one another. He had often begged them to live together in harmony, but without success. One day he called them together, and producing a bundle of sticks, he asked them each to try and break it. Each tried, with all his strength, but the bundle resisted their efforts. Then, cutting the cord that bound the sticks together, the Old Man told his Sons to break them separately. This was done with the greatest ease. "See, my Sons," he exclaimed, "the power of unity! Bound together by brotherly love, you can defy almost every mortal ill; divided, you will fall a prey to your enemies."

MORAL: *In unity there is strength.*

The Lion and the Mouse

A Lion, tired from hunting, lay sleeping under a shady tree. Some Mice scrambling over him while he slept, woke him. Laying his paw upon one of them, he was about to crush him, but the Mouse begged for mercy in such moving terms that he let him go. Some time after, the Lion was caught in a net laid by some hunters, and, unable to free himself, made the forest resound with his roars. The Mouse whose life had been spared came, and with his little sharp teeth soon gnawed through the ropes and set the Lion free.

MORAL: *Kindness is seldom thrown away, and there is no creature so small that he cannot return a good deed.*

The Fox and the Crow

A Crow, after stealing a piece of cheese from a cottage window, flew with it to a tree that was some way off. A Fox, drawn by the smell of the cheese, came and sat at the foot of the tree, and tried to find some way to get it. "Good morning, dear Miss Crow," said he. "How well you are looking today! What handsome feathers you have, to be sure! Perhaps, too, your voice is as sweet as your feathers are fine. If so, you are really the Queen of Birds." The Crow, quite beside herself to hear such praise, at once opened her beak wide to let the Fox hear her voice, dropping the cheese as she did. The Fox snapped it up, and exclaimed, "Ah! ah! my dear Miss Crow, you must learn that all who flatter have their own ends in view. And that lesson will well repay you for a bit of cheese."

MORAL: *Those who listen to false flatterers must pay the price.*

The Maid and the Pail of Milk

A Country Milkmaid was on her way to market, to sell a pail of new Milk, which she carried on her head. As she was tripping gaily along, she thought, "For this Milk I shall get a shilling, and with that shilling I shall buy twenty of the eggs laid by our neighbor's fine hens. If only half of the chicks from these eggs grow up and thrive before the next fair comes around, I can sell them for a good price. Then I shall buy that jacket I saw in the village the other day, and a hat and ribbons too, and when I go to the fair how pretty I will look! Robin will be there, for certain, and he will come up and offer to be friends again. I won't come round so easily, though; and when he tries to kiss me, I shall just toss my head and—" Here the Maid gave her head the toss she was thinking about. Down came the Pail, and the Milk ran out on the ground! And all her imaginary plans came to nothing.

MORAL: *Don't count your chickens until they're hatched.*